Juan Tuza and the Magic Pouch

Written and Illustrated by Francisco X. Mora

Highsmith PRESS

Fort Atkinson, Wisconsin

Para Katy
con muchos cariño
en su cumpleaños
F. Mora
1995

Published by Highsmith Press
W5527 Highway 106
P.O. Box 800
Fort Atkinson, Wisconsin 53538-0800

The paper used in this publication meets the minimum requirements of American National Standard for
Information Science - Permanence of Paper for Printed Library Material. ANSI/NISO Z39.48-1992

About the Author
Francisco Mora was born in Mexico City in 1952, where he studied traditional and contemporary art with some
of Mexico's most influential artists. Later he continued his studies in Europe and the United States. With bright
colors, mythical creatures and Mexican folklore, he creates a whimsical world of fantasy that subtly teaches about
reality. His writing and illustrations are interpretations of his dreams, memories and past, which draw heavily on
his childhood recollections of the sights, sounds and flavor of his Mexican heritage.

Library of Congress Cataloging-in-Publication Data
Mora, Francisco X.
        Juan Tuza and the magic pouch / written and illustrated by Francisco
Xavier Mora.
                p.   cm.
        Summary: As a reward for their good deeds and hard work in the
Mexican desert, Juan Tuza the prairie dog and Pepe the armadillo receive
a magic bag, which produces anything they need.
        ISBN 0-917846-24-9 (alk. paper) : $15.00
        [1. Prairie dogs--Fiction. 2. Armadillos--Fiction. 3. Magic--
Fiction. 4. Deserts--Fiction. 5. Mexico--Fiction.] I. Title
PZ7.M788185Ju   1994
[E]--dc20   93-34505
                                                    CIP
                                                    AC

Exhausted after a hard day's work Pepe the Armadillo and his partner Juan Tuza, the prairie dog, were just sitting down to eat dinner. They were in the excavating business. They loved to dig! They were sure that someday they would find a buried treasure.

"If I found *un tesoro*," said Pepe dreaming, "I would have a feast at my dinner table. I am tired of eating radishes and soggy weeds for every meal."

"If I found a treasure, I would buy a golden brush to use on my fur all day long. Then I would appoint you as my counselor, and you would wear a glittering suit of jewels. But best of all, I would build a house that has a hundred holes. You and I would be the lords of these hills!" added Juan.

Cuás, cuás, cuás sounded at the entrance of Juan and Pepe's burrow. Who could it be knocking that way?

"It's me, your landlord," said Memo *el Tlacuache*. As the possum brushed the dust off his dirty, torn coat he explained the reason for his visit. "I am here for the rent, and if you don't have it, I will kick you out of your cozy little home."

"Please, Memo, don't throw us out." pleaded Juan. "We'll get the rent somehow."

"If you don't pay me tomorrow, I will see that you
spend the night sleeping under the stars, ha, ha, ha!"
said Memo as he turned and left.

"Tomorrow I will go to *el mercado* and sell the radishes that we have collected from digging. With the money I earn, we can pay the rent," said Pepe.

"*Está bien*," said Juan, reassuringly. "While you go to the market, I will go to *el desierto*. Maybe I can find another place for us to live. Maybe I will find a treasure! Everything will be fine. Don't worry," Juan told Pepe.

Early the next day Pepe and Juan went off in opposite directions, both in search of their "treasures," wishing to each other "*buena suerte*," good luck!

After hours of looking and thinking as he walked in the desert, Juan sat down to rest under a *nopal*.

Suddenly, from behind the rocks, Juan heard a voice crying for help. "*¡Ayuuúdame!*"

The prairie dog rushed to see what was wrong. To his surprise he saw a great coyote with his hind leg trapped under a rock.

Even though Juan was afraid of coyotes, he never refused to help anyone. "Don't move. I will help you," Juan reassured the coyote.

Juan dug right and left and made a hole for the big rock to topple into. As the rock fell, it released the coyote's paw and he was free.

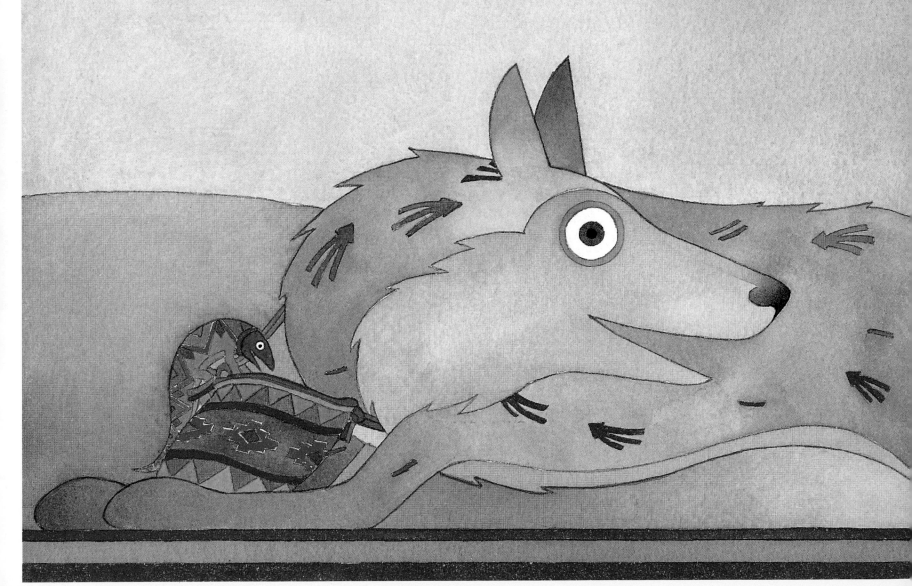

"*¡Muchísimas gracias!*" said the coyote.
"To thank you for your help, I will give
you this bag. It is magic. If there is
anything you want or need, just ask the
bag for it."

As Juan started to thank him, the coyote
disappeared into the desert.

"That was no ordinary coyote," thought Juan. "He gave me *una bolsa mágica*. It must have been the Great Spirit!"

At home, Juan was too excited about trying the magic bag to wait until Pepe returned.

"Magic bag," Juan said, "I would like a little sack of corn." And baboooom! Right in front of his eyes appeared a HUGE sack of corn.

"Magic bag," Juan said, "I would like a little sack of beans." And baboooom! Right in front of his eyes appeared a GIANT sack of beans.

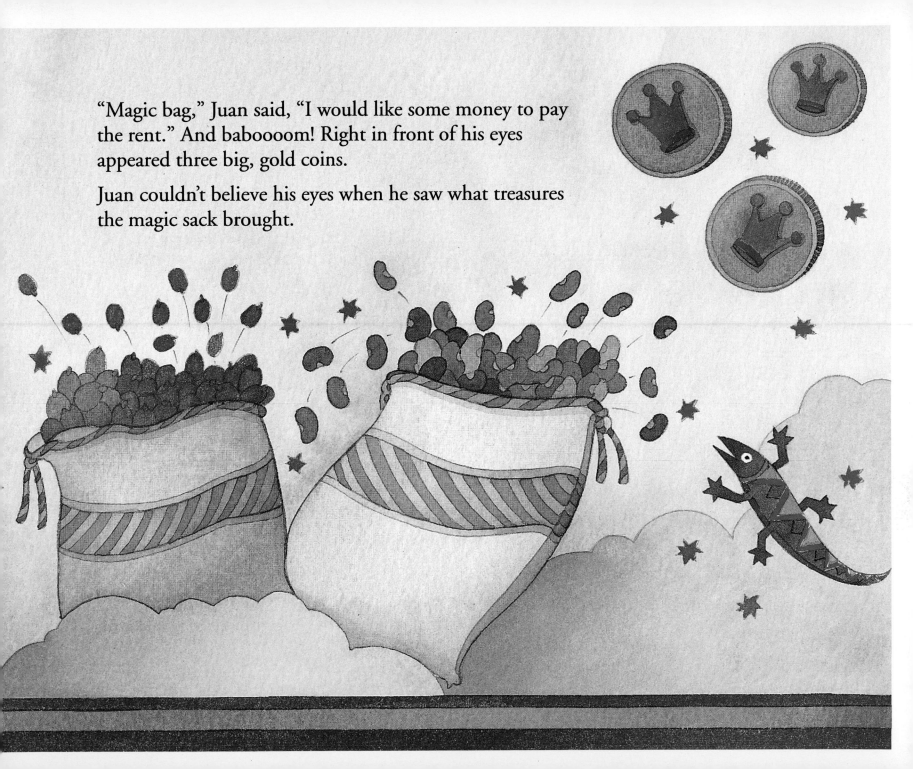

"Magic bag," Juan said, "I would like some money to pay the rent." And baboooom! Right in front of his eyes appeared three big, gold coins.

Juan couldn't believe his eyes when he saw what treasures the magic sack brought.

Suddenly, Juan heard *cuás, cuás, cuás*.
"I have come to collect the rent you owe me,"
yelled Memo the landlord.

"Please come in *señor*," answered Juan. "I
have your rent money."

When Memo the Possum saw the large bags of
corn and beans and the gold he became very
suspicious of Juan. "Where did you get all of
this," asked Memo greedily. "You must tell
me! I must know where you got all of this!
Hurry, tell me!"

"I got it all from *la bolsa mágica*," replied Juan.

"The magic bag?" "What magic bag?" asked the Possum.

"The one that the Great Spirit gave me for helping him this morning," answered Juan.

But before Juan could explain how he helped the Great Spirit, Memo demanded to know where to find him so that he could have a magic bag for himself. "If you tell me Juan, I promise never to bother you and Pepe for the rent again!"

"You will find the Great Spirit over that black hill, behind the cactus," Juan explained, as he pointed in the direction toward the market.

In search of the Great Spirit, Memo ran away as fast as his legs would go.

Meanwhile, for Pepe, it was a long day at the market. He wasn't able to sell the radishes and soggy plants. At least he traded some dry radishes for a cup of honey. Happy but tired, Pepe began his journey home, with his cup of honey and his bag of leftover radishes.

While Memo the Possum was running up the hill looking for the Great Spirit, he didn't notice Pepe coming down the hill carrying his jar of honey and bag of radishes.

¡CRAC! They crashed into each other, and everything went flying in different directions.

Pepe, covered with honey, landed in a pile of dried tumble weeds. When he stood up to brush himself off, Pepe looked like a monster. He looked terrifying!

Not recognizing Pepe the Armadillo, Memo said, "I am sorry for running into you Great Spirit. Are you hurt? Can I help you?"

Pepe was too surprised to answer him.

"Well, now that I have helped you, will you give me *la bolsa mágica*?" demanded Memo.

"What *bolsa* do you mean?" asked Pepe, still not sure what the Possum was talking about.

"You know which one. Just give it to me," Memo demanded again.

"I don't HAVE a *bolsa*. I just have this bag," Pepe told him as he showed him the radish bag he took to the market.

"That must be the one! Give it to me," the Possum demanded and pulled the bag away from Pepe. Before Pepe could protest, Memo ran away.

Tired, sore and covered with honey, Pepe finally
arrived home. To his surprise, their little house now
had a hundred holes! At the entrance, Juan Tuza sat
in a chair grooming himself with a gold brush.

Pepe suddenly didn't feel so sticky and dirty anymore. He looked down and saw that he was wearing a sparkling suit of jewels!

On the other side of the black hill, Memo the Possum was ordering the bag over and over to give him gold, pearls and emeralds. But the only thing the bag kept giving him was old, dried radishes!

Glossary of Spanish Words

ayuuúdame (a yóu da may)
please help me!

una bolsa (oó nah bówl sah)
a bag

buena suerte (bwéh na swéar tay)
good luck!

¡crac! (crack!)
the sound of a big crash

cuás, cuás, cuás (quahz, quahz, quahz)
the sound of knocking on the door

el desierto (L deh zee ér toe)
the desert

mágica (máh hee ka)
magic

el mercado (L mer cáh doe)
the market place

muchísimas gracias (moo chées ee mahs
                            grah sée us)
thank you very much

nopal (no páhl)
cactus

señor (sen yor)
sir

un tesoro (oon tay sór oh)
a treasure

el Tlacuache (L tal quáh chay)
the opossum

Tuza (tóo zah)
the prairie dog